Dear Reader,

I am minded that beyond those halcyon days of youth a magic lingers still. Cast not by a sorcerer's hand, but born of expectations untainted by the realities of life. Such magic imbuing each with sense of self and the enduring belief we might a difference make.

As I write, I look to the world about. Not yet blinkered to the wonders that abound but seeing well the shadows we have cast upon this Eden; a timely portent that in the absence of care all things might find their end. Such thoughts undoubtedly influencing this tale of Loss, each character a parody of some you may have come to know.

Be you of youth or young at heart it matters not. This tale I wrote for you. That you may look to the past and a future yet unwritten for yours is the legacy upon which both might be well founded! Enjoy.

Stephan J Myers

June 28th 2012

Loss De Plott

Stephan J Myers

Published by Hershey Reese & Myers Ltd 2012

First published in Great Britain in 2012 by
Hershey Reese & Myers Limited
Reg. No. 7331321

A CIP catalogue record for this book is available
from the British Library

Paperback (b/w) ISBN: 978-0-9573225-1-6

To the memory of 'Harry' Hawden, in the shadow of Horatio. For a true kindness is never forgotten.

1. Mean Streets Linger

I have to mind an image from many years gone by, for I think this is where my tale truly begins. When heavy with the burdens of youth and not yet succumbed to the scourge that is acne and downy growth I came across a broadsheet of fine standing. Not one that would have readily found itself to our door had it not been for its thermal properties and honest Ron's penchant for deep fried fare. Though for that sorry confession, the memory lingers. Not with great clarity but with the nagging suspicion my life and such progress that I have made might have been set upon an altogether different course but for that chance viewing.

Not that I knew it then but with the enlightenment often born of hindsight I can draw no other conclusion for mine were the mean streets where the ways were rank and narrow; houses wretched in their decay and the slipshod embraced ugly in a fest of moral decline. This I tell you not so that you may cast aspersions upon my character but that you may know the odds of that image finding me.

Marred not by the fare it served to warm but standing out in sheen and text so as to draw my interest and as monument to those mad men of furtive seduction who had crafted it so. Before my eyes young graduate sorts with smiling faces spoilt not by avarice or squandered expectation, sharp suited and booted with mortarboards and robes afore a glass monolith to corporate endeavours, with such trappings of success that might be conveyed by the cunning inclusion of jet plane and fast car.

It was my intention to draw you such an image yet there is devil in the detail that remains elusive and mine is not a hand for finer art, though I hope you find my dubious mortarboards at the least recognisable for what they purport to be and it will not prejudice you against further renderings I may make. It might also be prudent to add that all this was, of course, before the advent of age discrimination!

For whom that advert tolled I do not recall. Nor the exact text, but my memory leans towards snippet proclaiming 'excellent salary, rewarding career and personal development with a concern that prized its people'. And there was, though a rarity in these present times, some spiel about generous pension and 'a job for life' but to be honest those mad brokers of interest had me ensnared at the mention of coin and fleeting notion that excellent reward meant a sporty car and escape from the dross which seemed then to be my lot.

Should I appear shallow upon such comments then I fear I have misled and must apologise lest you reap the wrong impression, though it seems to me an inherent risk when one is being candid. In truth, it being betterment I aspired to, for as a role model honest Ron did sorely lack. In all ways a man might be measured for his only concession to the opinions of others and taller standing were none too subtle heel lifts that gave a peculiar lilt to his gait.

What path I might then follow to more lofty pursuit had not crossed my mind, at such a young age, but undeniably something in that picture did connect. I had not the foggiest idea what I was going to be but clueless and untested I knew for sure that I would scale the corporate ladder and realize much vaulted rewards. Though honest Ron, who on this occasion I will grudgingly concede was my father, called it working for the man and more derogatory he could not have been when I thought to save that image. Decrying the lives of the privileged few from his kitchen pulpit, who knew little of honest graft, whilst extoling his own shady code which required much fawning over the unsuspecting who engaged his ever changing repertoire of trades.

"Honest work too good for you?" He asked as he made rough of my image with a well mauled saveloy. Though that might well have been rhetorical in essence for I never quite came to fully understand what he meant by honest work and there can be no doubt our interpretations were worlds apart.

To be fair-minded he did endeavour to enlighten and attire me accordingly, doggedly referring to me as his apprentice one summer long. Though his inspiration was more Dickensian with an eye to cheap toil with I a sullen participant and not good for trade, with my return to school mutually welcomed.

I knew then that working for someone who proclaimed one thing and made good on another was not for me. Wanting more than ever to work for the company that made much promise of limitless opportunities, to be what honest Ron, with some loathing, referred to as a suit and it was to that end I remained focused. Though had I set myself upon an easier path it is entirely possible these words may never have found you, for an academic I was not and thus sorely suited to the task ahead of me.

I did however, throw myself into all subjects with some aplomb and for the most made the required grade. But it was to be my good fortune that the appliance of mathematics and science came hardest of all, for it was the somewhat limited career choice afforded by such that proved the turning point in my life. So much in fact that upon arrival of the obligatory two week work experience placement in my fifth year I was at a loss as to where my corporate life would begin. And it must remain a continuing point of moot, that with ill intent honest Ron did for me what hard work alone could not. For still bent on finding me that 'honest work' he did arrange for a 'wakeup call' courtesy of a sprawling industrial hive with Machiavellian undercurrents where fortune did turn towards me. And though I beg you not put much stock in harsh words I was admittedly relieved when the Union Steward deemed me unable to 'punch my way out of a wet paper bag' and forbade my presence upon his shop floor.

Unwanted but not downtrodden I was drafted then into personnel and a more serious group of people I had never met. Suited and booted it seemed to me they had been rough cast in some generic corporate mould, bereft of spark and though noticeably lacking in dynamics they subtly redeemed themselves as Knowledge Ninjas, skilfully weaving their way through the corporate ranks, information their currency of choice. If they didn't know it, then in the simplest of terms it wasn't worth knowing and by the end of my placement I was hooked and truly linked in to the wheeling and dealings of inner management and surely en route to a corporate career.

2. An Indulgence Begged

There are some tales told that beggar belief and might, if truth be told, cast doubt over the sanity of the teller. Indeed I fear you may come to question mine for I must now take what will appear a monumental step change in this tale, though in truth I can think of no other way to tell it and your indulgence I must here beg. In return I promise all will become clear and at some point along this path we traipse the proverbial penny, of which is often spoken, will tumble with a resounding and somewhat symbolic crash. But, it is by necessity that I must first introduce you to the strangest character I have ever met. Her name, one that you will soon know well and the circumstances of our meeting, which I am sure you will agree, were somewhat stranger. So much that I had reason to consider my own dear marbles and thought a picture would help explain why!

As you can see, I first made her acquaintance from what I mistakenly took to be a hospital bed (the rather ungainly and oversize feet being mine!). Though in truth I had no idea how I came to be there. My memories beyond recall, and I am sure you can imagine my surprise to find the first thing I saw upon waking was a somewhat slight and peculiar young woman simply sitting on what appeared to be a clock face, afloat in mid-air as though it were the most natural thing in the world. Even more so when she asked in a quirky little voice, "What ......does it look like?"

"I'm sorry?"

"What does it look like?" Well of course in my much flummoxed state I had no idea what she meant. It seemed like sanity had indeed abandoned me or else she had well and truly lost the plot. A point to which I will, by necessity, soon return.

Closing my eyes and covering them with the palms of my hands I felt sure what I was seeing was the result of mind altering medications! But, rub as hard as I might, when I opened them again she was still there. Staring wide eyed and tongue tied my thoughts turned to celestial harps, but I could feel the bed sheets drawn tight around me and felt confident there was a far more rational explanation.

As though reading my thoughts she gingerly placed her feet upon the floor, as if the experience was an unusual one to her and smiled in that particular way Doctors do to reassure their patients that everything is okay. When I finally found my voice, albeit somewhat faltering, I asked of her that most obvious of questions, "Where............ am I?"

Perhaps, given the manner of our meeting, I should have asked from whence she came. Though somewhat absurd it did come to me in that instance, that if I was to resolve the mystery of my peculiar circumstances, it would be her questions to be first answered.

"Please tell me ......what does it look like?"

I was about to tell her I understood not what she wanted of me when against all logic an image of a door came to mind. Not a very elaborate door, just plain blue with a rather wretched looking black knocker and the number seven dangling by a rusty screw, which was long past being useful.

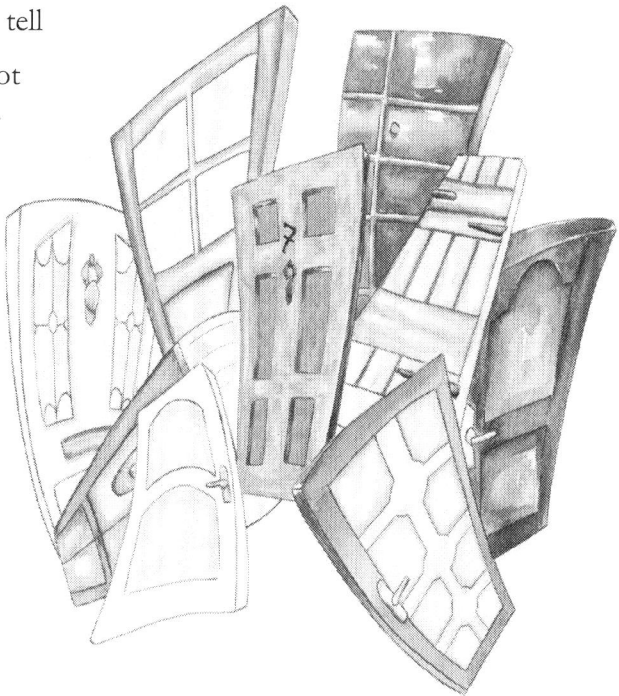

"No not that one," she said in the way one might speak to an indolent child. "That's where you grew up. Show me the other one."

Astounded that she could apparently see my imaginings our encounter had become infinitely more bizarre and wondering if she could read my thoughts as well I sent a few choice words in her direction but got no reply and immediately felt guilty. After all, she had solicited my help with a please, so I told her as politely as I could,

"I don't know what you want."

It was clear to me from the little furrows that formed upon that demure brow that this door I had apparently seen was of great import and when she said in that quirky little voice, "I will know it when you see it." I felt absurdly compelled to find it for her.

Suddenly an endless parade of doors came to mind. There were thin doors and wide doors, white doors and black. Doors with glass a plenty so that one could see who was on the other side and doors of hard lumber with tiny panes that a viewer might only just make out what lay beyond. Where I had seen these doors I could not recall but, as each one came to mind my new acquaintance would make a limp smile and shake her head. And still unsure of what it was she sought, my thoughts turned towards invention, showing her then an image of a revolving door. She thought on that a little longer as though unsure of what I was showing her before giving me a rather more generous beam, as though I had lightened our labours with a joke.

To be honest I think we were both becoming a tad frustrated when I suddenly realised that none of the doors I had shown her had been with keys.

"Yes, yes!" she said quite excitedly. "Show me the one with the key."

Of course, all the doors I'd shown her had needed keys but it was equally true that I didn't have the keys to many, if not all of them. So I did something of which I am not too proud and invented one, it arriving in my mind with bells and whistle. A gigantic door made of shiny steel with mirrored glass and a handle as big as my arm that I might only reach if I were to stand on the tips of my toes and there, below the handle, a key. For a brief second I thought I had gone too far but I was astonished to see a smile rivalling that of a Cheshire cat spread across her face. A beguiling radiance to her features did it bring.

"That's it. I knew you could show me it," and then leaning towards me she asked in a truly mischievous tone, "have you turned the key?"

"Why?"

"Because where I come from, everything is always so much more interesting on the other side!" With that the point upon which she turned on her shiny red shoes as if to leave, when it suddenly struck me she had not offered her name. Turning back she seemed to delight in stretching the moment, her fingers twirling an errant strand of hair as though deep in thought. It was then, I remembered, one should never make assumptions.

"You can call me Loss De Plott."

And that is how it all began!

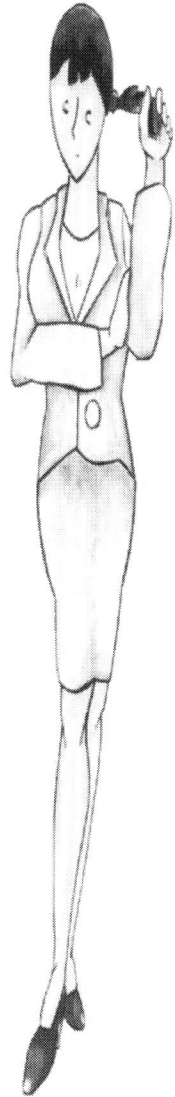

3. Words Without Meaning

It was with some haste I became reconciled to the strangeness of my little oubliette and that Loss De Plott knew infinitely more of me than I about her. Though much longer did it take to figure out where I was and from where it was she came from. Of the room I can say little other than it was painted in a sunny shade and was never cold. I had a little bathroom to meet my needs. Food would appear from apparently nowhere as and when my tummy grumbled and though meagre to look upon I never had cause to complain. And upon the wall just to the right of where I had first seen Loss was the number seven.

From a solitary window I could see the bluest sky I had ever known and more trees than I could ever count, but not a single sound could I hear. Had there been more than a pane of glass I would have certainly flung it wide; or a door then I would have surely ventured out. Though odd as this may seem I never once considered myself to be a prisoner of anything other than circumstance. In fact I had the most extraordinary sense of relief about me, which offered paltry explanation for my waking in fair semblance of a hospital bed!

Over the days that followed the sun would rise then fall to the moon and I learnt the rules of common physics held no sway. I never saw Loss come and go for as I have already said the room had no egress that I could see. Rather she would disappear and reappear in the blink of an eye in that corner, each appearance heralding subtle changes to that place and the arrival of curios that I could not ignore. Random things that made no sense at first but bit by bit helped me solve the mystery of where I was. For instance, on the occasion of her second arrival she pointed at a book nestling precariously on a rather sorry looking bedside cabinet.

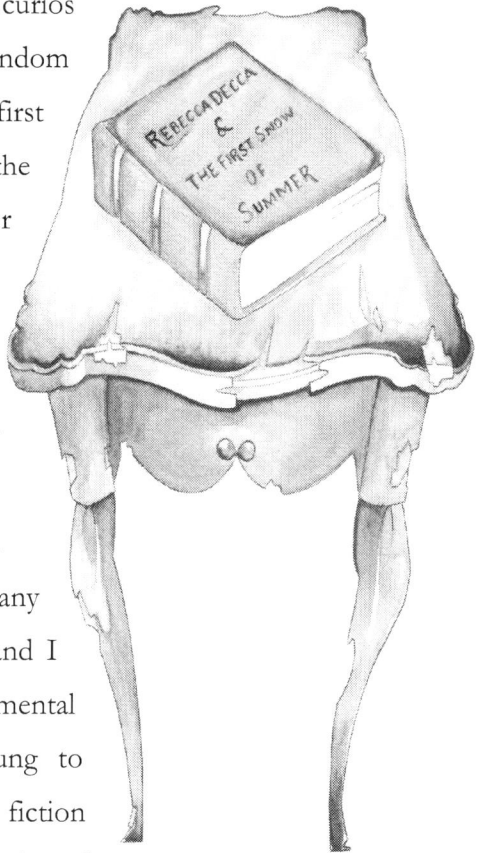

"You should read," she said.

"I do. I have many books...........somewhere," and I found myself doing a quick mental inventory of those that sprung to mind. All of dour content that fiction might not upon intrude and sad testament to a mind that new little rest. A staggering amount in fact that had they been of paper and bound would have surely filled many shelves and a cause of some concern for in the reading of so many what time had I for the pursuits of recreation? With it striking me in that moment this the book to which Loss pointed was something at odds to my usual inclinations. For case bound aside it was not of the sort I would have readily perused on an eReader or the net.

"Of these things you know, are they all from a book?"

"Well, yes………… and a Masters Degree," I added with a smidgen of indignation, for though the subject escaped me I could vaguely recall a ceremony for such where square grad caps had been thrown high.

"That's so funny. Imagine if your net was empty and all the batteries in your time died!" She said and upon which, all but fell over in a fit of laughter whilst I found myself contemplating what she had just said. Were we not from the same time?

Recovering her composure she shook her head a tad but offered no answer as she picked up that book. For a while she seemed lost in contemplation but I was not to be deterred. Everything about her was intriguing. Surely no one on earth might see my imaginings or hear my thoughts and the disc upon which she appeared, could there have been a stranger way to travel? Where did she come from, where were we, when? With it being then the most peculiar of ideas started to take shape along with image of a rather well known police box, painted in blue.

"Would you like me better if my skin was green or my ears pointed at the end?" she asked quite seriously. To be honest I didn't know and for a while we stood in awkward repose. Loss turning the book over and over in her hands as though the very feel of it were a source of comfort.

"Have you read the book?"

After a thoughtful silence she turned curious grey eyes toward me , and said very seriously.

"Words without meaning are not for reading," and with that she simply vanished leaving the book to fall to the floor. No longer in a pristine jacket but dog eared and poorly stained it looked oddly familiar. With image of a more morbid abode finding shape in my thoughts. In fact I was sure it had been left on a familiar desk many months before but I had never thought to read it. Had it been Loss who had left it there or was this simply a bizarre coincidence? Of the latter, I suspected not. There was nothing random about this place and I felt sure Loss would not return until I'd read the book from cover to cover.

It may be you have read that book and being familiar with tales of Rebecca Decca know that such suspicions of Loss I held were mercifully bordering on the right side of delusional. Thus, my sanity preserved and abandoned to my splendid solitude I began to read.

4. A Time Beyond All

Of that book Loss left I will little say, lest by chance you come to read it and a ripping yarn be spoilt. Making mention only of high adventure and much expectation of what has yet to come. But when that last page was turned and once more did it lay upon that sorry looking table, I was overwhelmed with a sadness for which words I could not find.

"One should never make promises that can't be kept."

My Loss was back and with her came the number six and a high back chair. Not one that wobbles when you are about a fidget or sticks to your back in summers heat, leaving muscles cramped at days long end. No! This was an exceptional chair of the finest leather with sumptuous wadding and a swivel base, that a statement did it make. A chair for contemplation, perhaps a chair in which promises might be made or contracts laid bare for the hammering. These things I do but speculate and though I knew for sure I had never seen that plush pew before, when Loss bade me sit I felt sure it wasn't the first time it had taken my weight. Knowing then, without reservation, that something of great importance I was about to learn.

"Can you see him? The man with the city slicker suit and the easy smile, he's so full of energy," she said.

And I could, for unlike my first encounter with Loss I knew exactly what she wanted from me. For much thought to words had I been giving. The expectations they raised, the imaginings of those who took them at face value and these thoughts had conjured up the image of the man we could now see. Afore doors of shining steel with sun high in the sky, his hand stretched out to welcome those before him.

"What a wonderful company you have joined. How lucky you are," I could hear him say as each one passed. A sea of expectant faces eager to join their colleagues on the other side. But as each new face passed him by it seemed his shoulders would hunch a little more as though an invisible weight was bearing down upon him. So many happy shiny faces passing him by that I lost count till eventually the only person standing before those doors was a raggedy man in a threadbare suit with stooped shoulders. No more a city slicker, as though an unseen trade had been made that did not in good conscience sit.

"Show me the other man," little Loss then said and a tad too eagerly for my liking. "The one on the other side of the door…"

But I couldn't. No matter how hard I tried to imagine the man on the other side all I could see were numbers and graphs flying past me in an increasingly maddening frenzy. The harder I tried the more that appeared. I thought she would be disappointed and was about to say how sorry I was when she smiled and touched my arm.

"Why can't people tell the truth?"

It was such a simple question to ask, the words barely a whisper, yet I knew we had crossed an invisible line. I had seen her laugh and I had seen her sad but in that moment I knew beyond any doubt that her story was much more important than mine and I would do anything I could to tell it. It had begun with words but it would be images and actions that defined the truth of what was said. For we all know it is in action that expectations flourish or wither will; it was with that very thought the room about us simply faded away and I had my first real glimpse of the mystery that was Loss De Plott.

In truth words may only conjure up a pale semblance of what I then saw. I have tried to capture it in a picture but you already know my skills as an artist are somewhat lacking. I wish it was not so, for all around me were the books of ages upon translucent shelves that one might imagine stretched to infinity and beyond. A fantastical library as one might imagine at the very end of time.

A limitless collection of books in all shapes and sizes, books written in languages long forgotten, others in languages to be yet spoken. All about us the wisdom and follies of man recorded in one Great Hall of Records. Each one identified by its title and date upon which it was published and not a computer to be seen. I suspect it was no accident that the book before me was the very book Loss had left for me to read. A simple date anchoring it in place,

beyond which was the works of countless years, centuries, millennia.

Had we lingered a lifetime I could not have known the truth of that place but there was a pressing question I had need to ask and could dally not, for abandoned here and there amongst the aisles were the very same discs upon which Loss now sat.

"Tell me, what year this place in which we stand?"

I suspect a simple yes or no would have made it too easy, but pulling me from my chair she set off at a pace which had me all but jogging to keep up.

"It's not far, but we can't linger. He won't like it."

Who this 'he' was, she would not say but true to her word it was not long before we came upon an open door and so heavy weighed my heart that for the briefest of moments I thought it broken beyond repair. Had you been there you would have first looked upon that ruined room. Those last frail remnants of a once grand fireplace bereft of flame, smelt the decay in those dusty volumes lining the walls of that soulless room, lingered perhaps upon that grieving armchair, yet still wondered what had touched me so.

"I thought one day I would read it."

I looked then to where Loss was pointing and in that moment saw everything as it had been. I saw titles in gold leaf flickering in the light of a roaring fire. I saw her as she would sit curled up in that easy chair with much contented smile upon her little face and it was this loss that touched me so, for to be given that which you may never know again must truly be the greatest loss of all.

I have drawn that image so that I may never lose it for as you know time is fickle and memories fade. That I am not an artist is plain to see but I fumble through as best I can with paint and water. Hoping to capture the essence of our tale and if all I can show you is a glimmer, then my greatest hope is that you will seek the depths in these frugal strokes of my brush.

There were, of course, many more books than I could possibly draw and the mantle is painfully lacking in detail, but if there is one thing you must always remember it is that Golden Scroll sitting atop of mantelpiece. Still bound in a green velveteen ribbon it was the one thing in that place she had refused to read and an anchor without which she was adrift. But here you will have to forgive me for although I wanted to ask why this scroll was so dear to her she had fallen into a reverie so deep; she seemed oblivious to my presence.

Seeking distraction I reached for one of those dusty tomes and had but brushed its surface when I realised these were not books as we know them, my fingers simply passing through cover as wraith like images sprung to life all about me. I saw the shadow of the books author hunched over a keyboard as midnight oil burned, heard the words forming in his mind, a child with his book in hand standing in a bookstore. For invested in every book were the hopes and fears of its author and incredible as this will seem, the captured thoughts of every person who had come to read it, their expectations and disappointments laid bare. Truly stunned I looked to Loss for answers and in that instance awoke once again in my little room.

5. Promises Given

Though Loss was not given to explanations, I was to learn something new with every awakening. Of course, it was quite frustrating at times but I soon learned to look to the small things, for with the right nurturing they might become things of substance.

There was no longer a bed in that room but a simple desk against window with five upon the wall and beyond now scattered here and there amongst the trees, were tiny buildings of drabbest grey. For what purpose I could not tell but it seemed to me that those trees were a lesser green and sky a duller shade of blue for their presence and when again I looked upon that desk, there laid a single pen and stack of crisp white paper.

"You should write a book," my Loss told me. "For that child in the bookstore and the grown up he will one day be, perhaps it would help him."

In truth I failed to see how a book that might only ever be considered fiction could help anybody and how would such a tale begin? Would I start with, "once upon a time I met a slip of a lass who floated in mid-air......" The very notion did have me laughing aloud. Though on more serious note what if my faculties proved below par and upon details of import did I err? For it would have pained me to know peeps thought of Loss, who I had strangely come to think of as my own, to be no more than a figment of my imagination and insecurities to the fore, what if no one wanted to read what I wrote?

"Oh!" Loss stared at me astonished. Then quite abruptly and without preamble she grabbed the pen and wrote in a spidery blue scrawl, 'once upon a time there was a man who dared write the world was not flat but round'!

It didn't escape my notice that she had underlined with heavy hand the word 'man' but of course she was right. Much of what is written requires a leap of faith, a willingness to suspend disbelief and allow expectation to flourish, to believe in something because it might be possible. But at the back of my mind, in the deepest darkest recesses where I doubt even Loss could reach, my fears still lingered. If I wrote of Loss I didn't want my

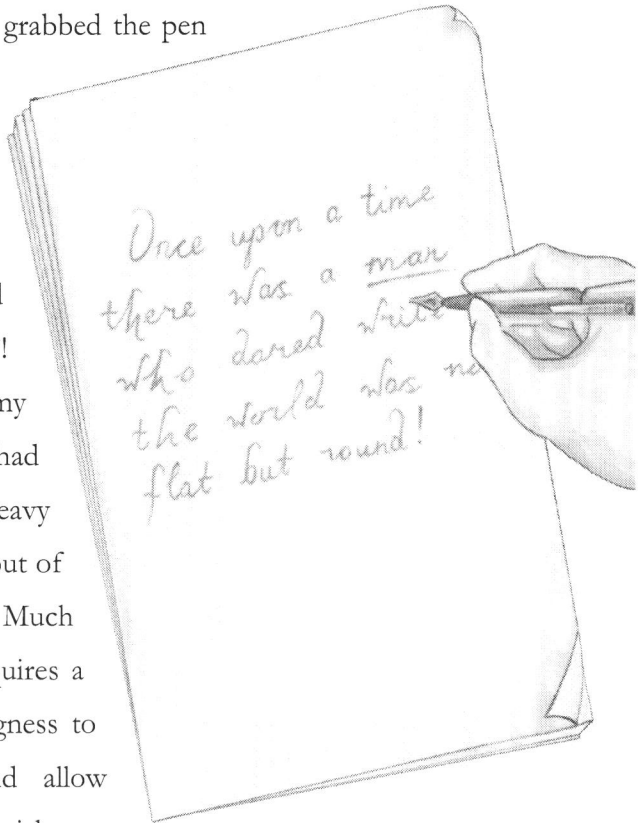

words to be taken lightly. I wanted people to know her as I had. If only I could have gone back to that Great Hall of Records. Would I have found a book upon those endless shelves that had captured the thoughts of those who read of Loss? Had she read such a book? Could we not just travel back there as we had done the day before? I had so many questions jostling for my attention that it was a while before I realised she was sobbing. Great rasping sobs and in between a few strangled words.

"I can't.........he took us back there to show you what I could not. I think you are meant to help me find my scroll, that's why I am here."

In truth, I didn't know what to say or do. I thought to console, to wrap my arms about her and make promises that might stop those tears from falling. To swear we would find that Golden Scroll. But honestly, I had not yet come to understand its true significance and such revelation that had neither of us in that little room by own volition had me rooted to the spot with my head a spin.

"But I thought....... you brought me here!" Such selfish words, when my Loss needed so much more of me! And once said I desperately wished I could erase them from her mind. I was about to say so but with her head turned from me, she continued.

"Heavens reach, I wish it was not so. Now you have learnt a truth such as this I am sure you wish yourself free of me."

As she spoke it seemed to me those walls about drew closer, as though seeking intimate knowledge of every sound and for the first time that wondrous little disc upon which she so often sat began to glow. Only around its edge, as though a halo and so very faintly that at first I thought myself mistaken. I had never thought it was for anyone

23

but my Loss to control, yet in that instant I realised how wrong I had been. I watched as she placed her hands upon its face and took a long drawn breath, closing her eyes as though listening intently. That body of light becoming so bright I was forced to shut my eyes with palms over, for fear my sight be lost.

An eternity it seemed before my Loss again spoke. It safe then to see about, but with distinct sense of urgency in voice she begged,

"Please, do not look at me. I'm a wretched thing to look upon when I cry." Then gently and no more than a whisper, as though afraid of being overheard, "I would have your promises but they must not be empty for I might never go home."

My poor little Loss, how fast we had become friends and like any friend of worth I could not be a bystander to her suffering. What did I care how wretched she might look? What did I care for my piffling insecurities when kneeling before me was a dear friend in need? I would not open my eyes but I could open my arms and when she came to me I rocked her gently and made the only promise of substance I could think to keep.

"This scroll that means so much to you......we will look for it together."

I did not see how I could say anymore for she would always know a lie, even one sugared with good intent and for the longest time we stood bound together in a clumsy silence. I not saying another word but waiting till she again found her voice, still so pitiful to my ears.

"I would only ask two promises of you."

25

Truthfully, there was nothing I could have refused her in that moment and two promises seemed quite meagre an undertaking.

"Anything, ask anything of me."

And I meant those words. Whatever she asked of me, no matter how daunting the challenge I would not let her down. If there was something I could do to stop her tears. To see her again in that library room as it had once been. Book in hand and fire ablaze. Then no more resolute in the face of challenge could a man stand!

"I would ask that you write of me......... a little every day." I made no answer for it was such a small thing to ask I wondered if she thought me less than able?

"No, no, not at all. I don't think anything of the sort. Words can only take a person so far but in challenging them you will find the truth. Please, this is not something that I ask lightly."

Still blind to my Loss and the room about me I could none the less hear a change in her voice, perhaps a little indignation that I might doubt the gravity of her request. I thought again of that Great Hall of Records, saw once more that authors solitary shadow cast by lamplight, felt the weight of torturous moments as he struggled to find words he would not regret. It then struck me that my Loss had asked not that I write a little of her for a week, not a month or even a year. She had meant every waking day! This would be no light undertaking, for neither pen nor keyboard came easy to me, a consequence of latent neglect in a man with no time for trivial pursuits. My Loss knew this and still she had asked.

Knowing then the gravity of it I could promise my little Loss nothing less than she'd asked and felt sure this brought an end to her tears for she had grown still within my arms, as though coming upon a quantum of solace. I thought then to ask of that second promise she would have from me, steeling myself as I did that it might make my first pledge pale by comparison but all she would say was,

"In time.........," and with that she simply faded from my arms leaving a strangeness for which I could not find words.

On opening my eyes the changes about me were plain to see. No longer was my little room of sunny disposition but drabbest grey much like the buildings beyond my window and though I cannot say it was any colder, it seemed to me the warmth had been leached away.

It was however the four upon the wall that irked me most. Not transformation met by waking eyes but bold testament to rules that were not mine to know; all hopes for time with Loss that might be anything more than brief, crushed in an instant. So quick a passing I would have to draw upon every minute detail if I was to keep my promise. More, I now knew that strangeness for the abyss it heralded and the irony of her name. Of course I would write of her and as my Loss already knew, I began there and then.

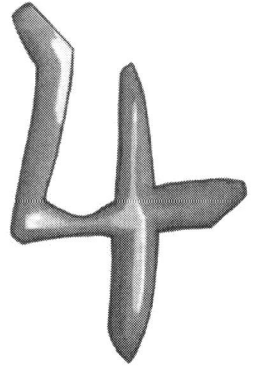

6. Questions And Answers

I had thought to be succoured by sleep before Loss returned, but in that I was fortunately fallacious for it seemed the sun had found a place to linger in the sky whilst I wrote and for that I was most grateful. So many words had I written. Many more pages with spindly blue scrawl than those without that I felt certain the dwindling stack of crisp bleached paper at my elbow would be long exhausted before her return. But her absence proved short and upon her reappearance she was minded to talk of many things, although she steadfastly refused to enlighten me as to whom 'he' was.

It does however seem inherent to any mystery that it may not be quickly solved. That between questions and answers there must always be an infernal drag upon the forbearance of the seeker and it is an unfortunate fact that I have never been the most patient of people. A trait Loss clearly shared! For once she had an idea she was like that fabled dog and its proverbial bone. It was clear to me then she was on a mission of enlightenment, upon which interruptions were to be frowned.

So I did learn with haste to ask few questions but listen more and though the reason for my own arrival in this odd little place continued to elude me, the voyage that had brought Loss to me gradually unfolded and much did I learn. Of that little study room she called home, that elusive Golden Scroll and the journey that brought us together. But here I must add a cautionary note for the more bizarre the truth the easier it is to dismiss as fantasy. I have certainly tried to capture everything she told me, so that you may find the verity in her words but such was her way to wander mid-sentence there are missives that upon first reading might appear have little resemblance to the subject in hand. It is possible I have made some errors, perhaps our times being so far apart there is meaning I have yet to unravel and of course she was given to asking the strangest of questions.

"Tell me," she said as though pondering upon a great dilemma. "In your time .... can a word once cast still be erased?"

It was a peculiar term she had chosen that drew to mind an image of fly fishing and seeing the smile spread across her face I answered without further consideration.

can a word once cast still be erased?

"Mostly, yes."

"Oh!" She said with a mere hint of haughtiness. "Then I wish it were still so. How lucky to live in a time where a simple eraser can right

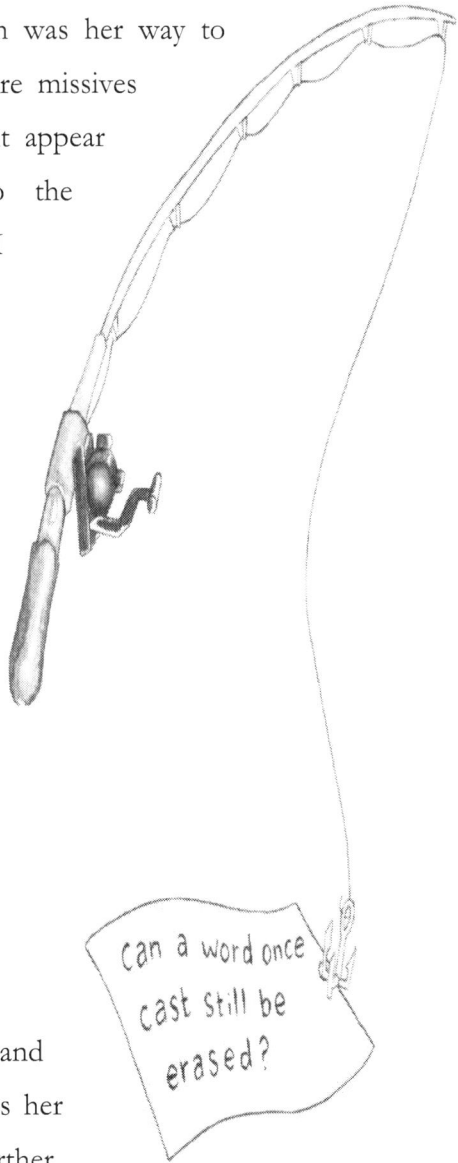

a wrong or words not ghost in machines where prying eyes may linger."

I saw then the ease with which I had been baited and the hook from which I might not easily wriggle. Such a clever little minx she was. As beguiling as a rose yet sharp as a thorn!

"I did say...... mostly."

"You did, truly. But what of those words not erased......how will they grow?"

I didn't answer. Sometimes she could be quite perplexing and in that moment I found my attention drifting beyond the window where the ugliest of flowers had begun to sprout between those drab grey edifices. Perhaps they are weeds I mused, for I had no green fingers and little practice in the care of gardens. But such ponderings proved fleeting for it was then, undoubtedly by pure coincidence, that Loss chose to tell me of the constant gardener. A strange fellow whom I will come to soon but first there are things about Loss I must tell you.

Though I often pressed for an answer, my little minx would neither confirm nor deny the year in which that Great Hall of Records resided and though I continued to think on it I came to consider more what she did in that place. It was not an easily undertaken enquiry for though she was given to asking many questions she seemed to have selective hearing when it came to enquiries I made of her. Rather it was the images she showed me and quite random snippets of information that helped enlighten me as to this enigma that had engrossed me so.

I came to know that for the longest of times she had taken great pleasure from 'his' books, coming to each with the unbound mindfulness that grownups seem sadly destined to lose. I had seen a glimpse of such in that room of hers and might rightly have assumed more from her presence in that extraordinary place, had my assumptions not then reduced her to exultant fits of laughter.

"What?" I mustered with my frustration clearly evident for it was beyond me how anyone could be so endearing and yet so vexing in the same moment.

"No one actually reads those books, at least not for pleasure!"

Suitably chastised I had hoped for an explanation but was instead reminded of the book she had left for me to read. There had been no rush of thoughts or wraith like images to overwhelm me. With a much travelled cover and dog eared pages it had been nothing more than it appeared. Despite an onslaught of technology that would have all books in the worlds libraries found upon the head of a pin and the marvellous workings of that Great Hall, there was still wonder to be found in well-thumbed pages and a magic to be worked by an open fire for one such as Loss.

I thought then that there might be times when loneliness would court her for it seemed to me the comfort to be found in a book may be finite. What then, when the last page has been turned, does one do to wile the time in the absence of others? I would have asked her but I was beginning to think words redundant and simply let the thought linger until she chose to speak of it.

"I wasn't always alone. People would come to me when they needed someone to talk to," and I wondered then if we had more in common than was immediately apparent. "It can be quite overwhelming caring for 'his' books, especially when 'he' has asked you to grow the very best words."

"You mean write?"

"No," she said. As if she were talking of something quite normal. "There was definitely a man who grew words. You know, like a gardener."

I certainly didn't. In fact I could not think of anything more ridiculous than a man planting words. Next she would be telling me the books, of which she was so fond, had fallen from the branches of trees!

"I didn't say he planted words. That's just plain silliness …he grew them from seeds. In fact, he grew the very first word that was ever spoken, by anyone!"

Such utter twaddle I thought but as she looked upon the still pen in my hand I felt my resolve wither. My Loss then taking a long deep sigh, as though she had just admonished a child.

"Really, how will we ever find my scroll if you aren't interested in the seeds it grew from," and verily did she refuse me another word until I put pen to paper.

7. A Most Constant Man

It was then I learnt of this grower of words. You might have thought him a very old man, dry as a stick and hunched with age but my little vixen assured me I was not much younger! High-shouldered and bony; he was not a man to mix well, for he was against idle chatter and had an air of pomp about him; for he was considered in high esteem. But a harder working man you might never meet for his every waking moment was dedicated to growing the best of words. Not toiling with rake and hoe in a great garden as one might think befitting that place, but in a little study much like her own. Though with a southerly aspect and an enormous window of arched design through which sunlight broke upon a solitary fey tree. And of such dainty proportions it might easily have been mistaken for bonsai.

Myriad were the number of such trees this constant gardener had grown, for as my Loss pointed out there were many thousands of languages spoken and more forgotten but each tree demanded exceptional care as they were capricious by nature and not given to easy bloom. Each grown from a single seed in a humble terracotta pot, many thousands might be sown and break soil only to wither by day's end. Every tiny sprouting a whisper of promise and cause for much remorse, that had this cultivator of note seeking solace from my Loss.

"I am a constant and patient man," he told my little teller of tales, "but there are times when I have known great despair. It is rare my tiny trees take root and even rarer for one to blossom but I have never let 'him' down," and patience being the staunchest of virtues he was in time rewarded with a hardier sprouting, that met days end with greater fortitude.

You might have thought such uncommon a happening cause for excitement but it was the point from which his constant nature might be truly tested and he met it with sombre countenance. Taking secateurs in hand he took a seat and from sunrise to sunset maintained a solemn vigilance.

For many days did he sit, watching that tiny sprig grow and harden into a trunk from which sprang the first of many minuscule branches. His eyes never once wavering from a task he seemed intent on keeping secret. But my agent provocateur would not be so easily deflected and in the absence of an explanation she resolved to join him in his vigil.

In time it found full form and began to show the first signs of blossom. But a few delicate buds at first that dallied parti-coloured in the morning sun as though wooing suspense and the continued attentions of its vigilantes, and had my Loss contemplating the origin of words. A point of mute upon which she would not later be drawn, for it was clear I had not been alone in courting scepticism.

It won't be long," her green fingered friend offered without

preamble. "Upon sunset I think," and for the first time in days he left his seat. Not to stretch or find relief but to throw open wide that great arched window before edging even closer with those secateurs. Beckoning my little voyeur forward he pointed to a single bud that had alone doubled in size and seemed possessed of a twitch as though making great preparations. No clue would he give as to what lay within, but upon exactly sunset those parti-coloured petals unfurled to reveal an offering that flouted her expectations. Not a word or even a flower of dazzling complexity but a blood red pearl tethered by a single gossamer thread spinning slowly before her. Staring steadfastly upon it, she at first thought it solid but as she watched, it shimmered and glistened, first in one part and then another. Fading to an ethereal hue only to show itself again, more distinct and spinning ever faster and in the very marvel of this, she could see countless gauzy tentacles as the very fabric of it began unravelling. But there was stranger still, for within those she could see fluctuating images, the likes of which she had not before seen. Constantly morphing, finding form then slipping into nothingness. Though she would not say aloud, she knew then the tree from which these seeds had come. There could be no thought without knowledge and only in original thought could the best of words be found, for a word may be no more profound or cry a greater truth than the first time it is ever spoken.

Lost as she was in her reverie she didn't see him wield those dark secateurs but her eyes followed that bloom of creation as untethered it took to a temperate evening sky, then fraught with curiosity she followed him to the window and looked out. Watching as in the blink of an eye it became a thing of gigantic proportions stretching from horizon to horizon before waning into the ether.

"It will return as the finest of words," was all he would say. Maybe for the tremor that stymied his voice or perchance no more was needed, for my Loss had seen the invisible and come to know the very origin of words.

"I so wish you had seen it, that I could show you but it was all so fleeting."

Truly I wished it so. I had followed her every word, my pen a feverish instrument that knew no respite yet no more than a pale incarnation could my discourse be. To have been gifted as my Loss, to see such a wonder through her imaginings, there was so much more I would know of this invisible world but such thoughts were laden by fatigues of the day.

"Perhaps if you close your eyes you will find it." I heard her words come soft and gentle as a whisper, but it was the vista beyond my window that held my attention. Where sun had abdicated to the rule of night with Morpheus stalking the weary and knowing then her already gone, I could do no more than give myself over to the inevitable.

8. Great Thespian Flare

For Loss, knowing the origin of words was to know her limitations and though I had come to think it a grand thing to know the thoughts of others, it had for her become a source of much torment. She had asked me how many times a word might be used before becoming so bastardised and twisted as to be but a pale semblance of its intended meaning. I had no answer, but I was not ignorant of the dilemma that vexed her so and was much aware that in eschewing those books of light for more mundane repose she had sought respite from dark qualms that had her doubting the veracity of that Golden Scroll. Though its significance and how she came to lose it still eluded me.

"I might have misled you.........a little." My muse was back with a non too convincing cough and a manner that wailed vulnerability for contrition did not suit her.

"Go on......" Shielded in nonchalance, less any show of sympathy had me played like a fiddle, I stood resolute in pursuit of the truth for much had changed in that tiny room and time was not an ally in seeking answers.

I learnt then of her arrival in the Great Hall. Itself a revelation of note for I had not considered my Loss being from anywhere else, though she assured me her reaction was not dissimilar to my own when first she arrived. And had 'he' not found her it was clear her tale would have been the sadder for it. I thought of dunking chairs and a hanging judge, such that it might bring a smile to her face but was met with a wan frown that found my demeanour wavering.

Of this 'he' who presented as saviour and Samaritan she would still not be drawn but she had put much stock in his goodwill and in that little study she had found a purpose for which her gift was well suited. She had already spoken of that constant gardener but there were many more who came to talk or simply sit if words failed them and in time she had come to call that place home.

"Had it not been for 'him' my life would have been that of a loathed and freakish thing," she confessed between little coughs, "and for a while I thought my new home perfect."

But the stronger her gift became the less her benefactor would visit and that had her considering the verity of promises he had made, for his were the only thoughts she could not hear. Never did he ask anything of her but knowing well the disparity between words and thoughts the more she considered deceit, for why would someone do so much and ask nothing in return.

"I had thought it a clever thing to know the thoughts of others but truly it is a curse," she did confess. For despite the goodwill of her patron, Loss had come to distrust his intentions and given her propensity for bluntness may have said as much, had it not been for the arrival of that Golden Scroll. The seal of that Great Hall of Records upon it and bound in a green velveteen ribbon it had appeared upon her mantelpiece in the way of things there, with a simple note that read, 'promises made good.'

"I thought to read it. But I was so wrapped up in the contrary nature of thoughts and words that no good could come of it and I resolved then to judge him according to his actions. I felt sure then 'he' would come visit me and see how much I trusted him. But he didn't come.........and knowing then the origin of words it set me upon a course of thought I could not undo. I tried......really I did but I had it to mind that he lied."

"So you read it?"

"Not exactly......," she said with a much shamed mien. "I burnt it!"

For sure, this was not the revelation I had been expecting and to be candid I was somewhat at odds with the notion such a trivial happening had led to so much angst. Surely such pledges might be rewritten, perhaps a simple apology. I had thought to hear a cutting

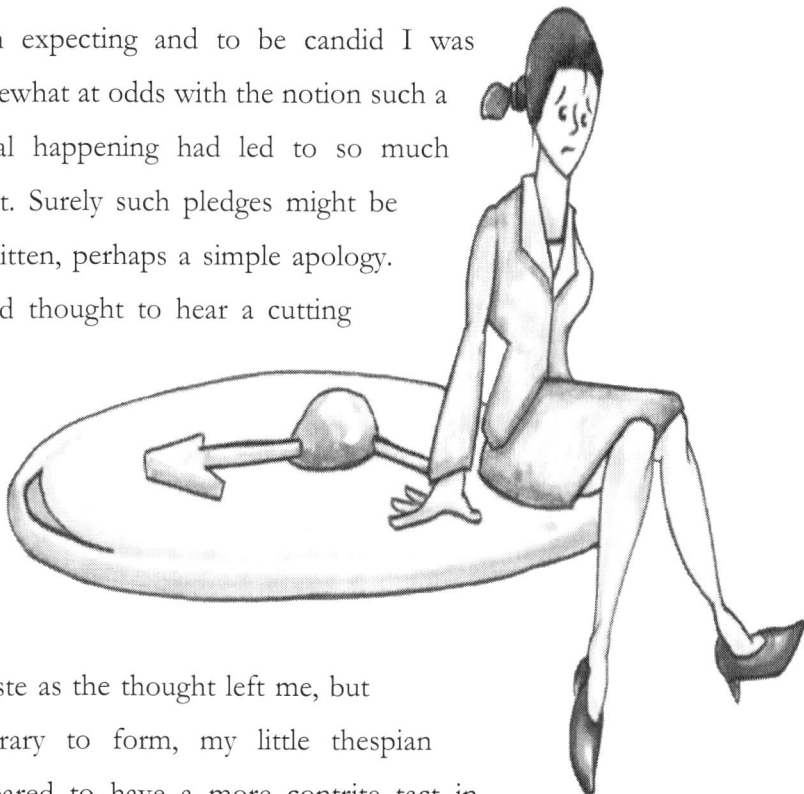

riposte as the thought left me, but contrary to form, my little thespian appeared to have a more contrite tact in mind which with her continued attempts to solicit a modicum of sympathy had me most befuddled!

"I did want to say sorry. Really I did, but he always came to me and no one knows how to find him............except the constant gardener and having learnt of my doing he was not inclined toward me."

Truly, with such slippery discourse she could have tested the patience of more saintly disposed than I and with my own bordering on threadbare I could wait no more. As well she knew, and it was with some aplomb that she delivered her swansong. Sitting on the edge of her disc, head hung in a parody of shame as she kicked at the air; she abandoned the little coughs in favour of a tremulous timbre barely higher than a whisper.

"How was I to know he had foretold my......... tribulations. Or that he had taken it upon himself to find the origin of those words. Perhaps if someone had told me that bloom was intended for my scroll............"

"The one you watched grow?"

"Yes, he took to its trail that he might be sure to know the true meaning of the thoughts and words it inspired......so I would not doubt him."

Still much baffled I felt as though I was wading through treacle with each considered revelation doing more to obscure the crux of the matter.

"I thought the same......I didn't understand why everyone was so angry till I thought to look within his books. I realised then the purpose of my scroll. Only the finest of words may endure, held higher than others because they have the power to bind thoughts to actions. But to stand so, they must return to their place of origin and be tethered........to a Golden Scroll."

I glimpsed then the gravity of such rash action as she had taken, but such thoughts struggled for expression and in the silence between us I looked to the changes I had met upon wakening. Those drab grey buildings no longer a mere blot on the landscape but a sprawling metropolis in the making. That numeral in decline again and the faintest tracings of a door frame upon far wall, a none too trivial development Miss De Plott seemed bent on ignoring!

9. A Measure Of Redemption

Considerably enlightened, I came to know that the best of words no longer bound might still be bandied about but in time come to be mere penuries of the thoughts that gave them form and as such might be used to lure and cajole without care for more lofty ideals. With that my considerations returning once more to first sight of that Great Hall and of those discs laying in careless abandonment. What then the consequences of such anarchy and maelstrom of displeasure that had one so beloved as little Loss cast from her home? Certainly this was not an enquiry that I made lightly but contrary to form my Loss was quite forthcoming.

"I had expected such but it was not at all like that," my Loss confessed. "I was younger and think seduced by vanity to think it all about me. When at last he returned and I thought to tell him how silly I had been, to beg his forgiveness, he would not have it."

"How could you have known, if I did not tell you," he had told my little object of happenstance, for he had thought to put things to right and was loathed to see her wronged on account of oversight. But in truth it had been no easy undertaking to follow a thread of such complexity when that for which he sought was anchored, what chances then when it was in the ether?

"Truly I could not let him right a wrong of my making for all around a great unravelling had begun and I could not stand to see the pain of it upon him when he had given me much. And though I begged him to take me with him 'he' would not be swayed." Beyond that no more on her departure would she say. Though it was clear to me then that she had taken it upon herself to put all to right and these events to which she alluded had touched all who dwelt in that place.

Seeing to it that her study was in good order and embers cold should latent spark add further woes, she made good her cherished books and left without note or farewell, perhaps thinking that in time he would come upon her trail. Considering not then of sacrifice but of a quest through which she might find a measure of redemption for the wrong she had done. My Loss so dogged in her determination that she might not be turned.

Again I pressed that I might know where that Great Hall resided but deftly did she parry my query and spoke in lieu of a world overrun by the machinations of a few who coveted dark design and the years which were history that lay before her. And I knew then that the boundaries of time, perchance space, as we have come to know them were no deterrent to the search upon which my intrepid trekker had embarked.

10. A Cold Chain Forged

As you might imagine, the passing of time had brought about many vagaries and hard pressed was I to reconcile such to this tiny earth as my Loss came to share them. Certainly, there were the fantastical predilections with which I may have sought to regale, that you might think me a person of good fortune to have been witness to, but there were as many to the contrary that cast a shadow over many much fancied predictions. Safer then to turn to the characters of those she chanced upon for in each were the malaise of consequence and the nexus of a paradigm shift that had begun with that Golden Scrolls demise.

To the first she was drawn, for he was a smith of words and the source of much lamentation and regret. I would have had him weak shouldered with a wisp of hair and long, lank, skeletal limbs behind a desk but the technology of that time pandered much to vanity and he had chosen a different persona with which to greet my Loss. Wide shouldered and lean, dressed in the colours of avarice, his hammer a beguiling pretence wielded in a parody of his vocation, his desk an anvil upon which he had forged many dark scrolls for the binding of wills.

"Hello," said my little inquisitor in expectation of a common courtesy. But the customs of that time dictated veneration before engaging in dialogue and he was minded to make her wait.

Taking his hammer to hand he raised it high, bringing it down on that much stained anvil with a ring that caused Loss a start. Not for steel upon steel but for the mournful wailings of the ruined and dispossessed that lingered in its echo; for much expectation and good will had been broken on the backs of his words.

"Such a sad sound," she mused and was met with a scorning.

"Argh!" he exclaimed as though it was the first he'd heard from her, "I thought I caught someone enter. So rare I get small people these days." Then setting aside his hammer he made a study of his work, making a great show, such that she would know it of the highest value.

"I think your furnace is dying," she ventured, for there was little warmth in that place.

"What, of course it isn't! Look how bright the flames are." And indeed they were, for it was all a grand illusion that she might not see the coldness of the deed upon which he made his coin.

Unperturbed my Loss turned to the room about her thinking that she might sit for a while but this smith of words was not given to good housekeeping and strewn all about were discarded scrolls that left little room for comforts.

"I had a golden scroll once but it fared poorly in the flames." Said my little mistress of understatement, for she was about finding common ground on which to bait him. "Perhaps if it had been black like these I would not be without it now."

"Ah." He said with a wolfish grin, "I see now that you are a teller of tales come to entertain me," for he had it to mind that golden scrolls were the stuff of fables. Told by those of a lazy disposition, long lost to the dreams of day, and no coin in my Loss could he see for the making.

"What is to be done with all these scrolls?" she enquired.

"Done? Why they are for the binding, a simple melding of pledges to wills given freely for good reward."

"Oh," said my little paragon of innocence, "I thought they might be broken."

"Broken? Never! A million such have I forged and not one ruined or I would a pauper be. There is no value in broken pledges. These though," and he gestured to a few about him, "are pledges made good, that I might smelt and make scrolls anew for there is decent coin to be made." Then taking tongs to hand he put his work to the flames.

Making a great show of pumping bellows until the coals in his furnace turned white before turning once more to his anvil, wispy tendrils of smoke curling about him as hammer rose and fell.

Intrigued by such a fanciful pretence my Loss lingered as words to scroll were welded and that folded a hundred times over so it consisted of countless paper thin laminations binding pledges to will in a pact of shadowy design. Within the rhythm of his labours a dark enchantment that called forth the spectres of those shackled by his doings. Coming first as confused wailings, then mournful and laden with accusations as those wisps of vapour about him took phantom forms, each one connected with a thousand thoughts bereft hope and joy. The fountain of misery within each founded upon contracts brokered by that smith of words.

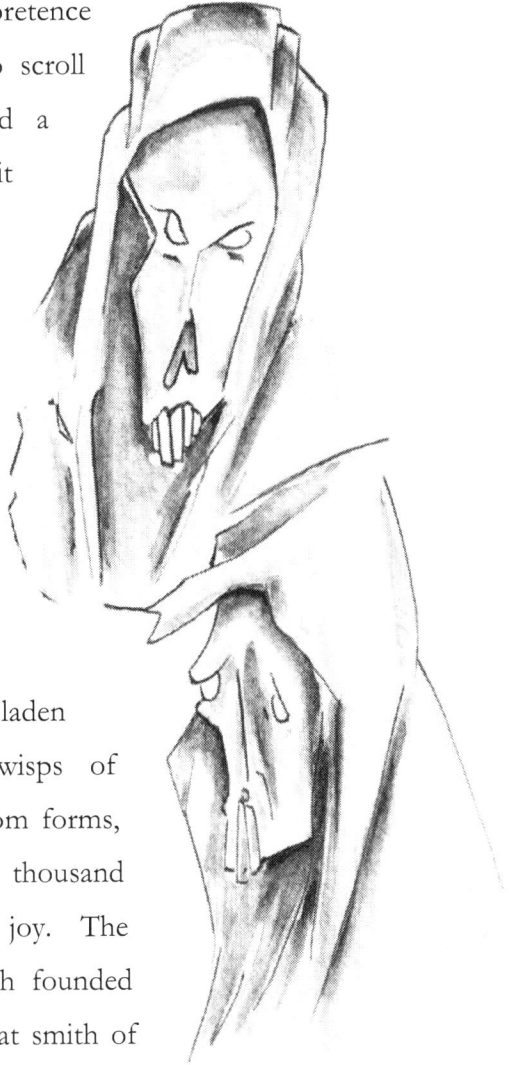

In truth I would have been hard pressed to stand my ground, but my Loss was drawn less to those apparitions than to the demeanour of her host who gave no inkling as to the happenings about him. Seeing then the mantle of his persona for the distraction he so wantonly embraced.

Plunging his devilish works into water he wiped his brow and turned towards her as those wraiths simply faded to nothingness. Considerations of self, so consuming that no thought of worth could she find. But she had glimpsed the chain he had forged. Link by link, cold and corrosive, shackled by his own free will to coin that fuelled his vanities. And only then did he let the grand deception fall.

If you recall I would have had him weak shouldered with a wisp of hair and long, lank, skeletal limbs. But in that I would have been too generous, for a far more wretched thing was he to look upon and hard was it to imagine that such a loathsome creature might find redemption.

"They were but shades of things come and gone," he offered with a toady shrug and much wringing of his hands, but my Loss was already in the wind. His words a haunting echo she would not easily put aside.

11. Times Long Lost

Beyond that forge of dark despair my Loss did flit across many years, where undeniably saddened by her encounter with that smith of words she took sanctuary in a solitary cloud. There divorced from the world and its many distractions and to dark thoughts she might have taken but for the most unlikely of diversions. I thought of cherubs and other celestial bodies, for little would have amazed me then, but it was in a weird melding of myth to such sciences as then prevailed that my little aviator extraordinaire found respite. Seemingly cobbled together from man made things so as to resemble a great golden bird with feathers tattered and furled, it announced its arrival on the wings of the wind with a questionable squawk and a landing that left much to be desired. Upon which it began strutting back and forth with a sombre shaking of its head.

"No good. No good."

"Hello." My Little damsel of melancholy said politely, and not at all surprised to be in the company of a talking bird, "won't you sit a while and tell me what troubles you?"

"I fear I am beyond help," that bird then said, "for I am soon to be extinct."

Thinking the bird a product of some weird science and a more apt term might be defunct, my Loss thought to state the obvious yet upon reflection decided to play along; for she was in need of company and thinking a good yarn might be spun she asked, "What do you mean extinct?"

"Why are you here?" the bird asked.

"I'm searching for something. What do you mean extinct?"

"Few care for consequences," said that golden bird. And beckoning my accidental host to the edge of their shared perch bade her look upon monstrous monoliths of industry that had made a new face upon our little earth. Their signage bold and brazen as they sought ever greater heights, for in their raping the sky was all that remained.

"Till the last was felled I made my home in tall trees so that none might see me. Then to the tops of mountains, shrouded in cloud, but rude stone cast in shadow are they now and it was to the clouds I came last. Each one leeched from the sky till this last one remains. Coin and promises, that's the only thing that interests them, tell me which do you seek?"

"Neither," said my much vexed Loss. "I seek nothing more than a thought. Please tell me what you mean by extinct." For strange as her companion did appear she felt sure he might be remade.

"It comes to all in time but when my last breath is drawn there will no more ....like me," said that bird with some thespian flair.

"You mean to die?"

"Yes."

"But you're not a real bird," my Loss blurted forth. "Surely you could be repaired!"

Falling silent the bird stared at my Loss with clear kind eyes, for she had only spoken of what she knew. But it had come to know reality for the paradox of time it was and had seen such made many times over. How then to reveal the truth with time so unforgiving and words prejudiced by what is known and gone before.

"Have you seen many real birds?" it enquired.

"Not to talk to," my Loss said with a modicum of indignation. "But when I was younger I would watch them in flight and think how wonderful it would be to dive and soar amongst the clouds."

"And here you are," her golden winged companion said. "A fanciful notion made real, yet there is a world below us that knows only barren skies and would think you upon this disc the creation of a much touched mind."

Turning then to the east, where the rising sun had left a streak of fiery red, my Loss saw the changes about her and for not the first time she had cause to wonder how many that now marred our little world were of her doing. For in truth she had read little of history before the Great Hall of Records and knowing not how that enigma came to be could not find a measure for the unravelling she had brought about.

"I think I was wrong," she told her faux feathered companion, though on what she did not expand and the bird taking her words as a sign of contrition thought to turn such to a common good with a favour sought. Not a mere token but to be given freely from the heart, for the sun was rising fast and upon its Zenith there was an end to make.

Spreading wide then one golden wing to rake the air, shimmering imageries did it leave in its wake. Of a great bird, not golden but of the deepest crimson and upon the air coming a scent that whispered of heady spices and sultry winds that had lingered long before the ravages that were time. Of great nations built high on common cause, the ruins of decadence brought low in the shadow of its passing and black robed figures with their collars turned.

"The time for innocence lingers only in shadows now, all myths dispelled, yet in hope we are one minded." Might have been its final words for to flight it then took. Mighty wings lifting it ever higher as the sun made its peak.

Wait, my Loss made to cry for she knew then the truth of that bird. But in knowing she would be the last to see its flight she was truly struck dumb as to the heavens did it soar. Growing not smaller but ever larger, drawing the heat of the sun to its body as gold did turn a bloody crimson and flames took hold.

And that favour asked? A legacy of life left upon her disc that with the greatest care might nurture hope, and two simple words carried on its dying breath.

"Remember me."

12. Patron Of The Arts

Of that entrusted to my little guardian she would not speak but the toll upon one so slight was surely heavy, for it was to the shadows she had taken, seeking myth that she might find hope. The years rolling back so that which had been so overrun gave way to green spaces where one might linger, if the mood was upon them, and there came a time when she could do nought else.

Not much to shout about in that place she chose, but trees might still be found and it being a time of holiday my little mingler found herself borne in a flushed and rowdy group towards the sound of much laughter. With fate dictating it be not at all generous but weighted by ridicule and the object of such raucous discourse, a man without a voice. Not dumbstruck but so constrained by his art for he was a mime man, taking the invisible and making it visible through gestures and movements of his body. Though it seemed not one person there deemed his silent show worthy of their applause.

"We can't hear you!" Cried a much sloshed heckler, and loudly did they guffaw, then another, "such a silly fellow!" But being thoroughly

good natured, and not much caring what they laughed at, he encouraged them in their merriment till in time they grew bored and strolled away. There to mix with other groups where bawdy words bolstered ego and made good their standing.

"I had read much of Mime, but had never seen a mummers play," my little patron of the arts did tell and minded was she to linger. His one solitary spectator taken to a grassy knoll where she could lay and watch the last of his silent tale unfold. Finding as she did that she was drawn to expressions and gestures that transcended words alone. In her telling, my own thoughts drawn to aged film noir. Flickering in the darkness of a silent movie hall, where within actions spoke the volumes that words alone could not. Where a spell once woven might only be ruined by the bounds of imagination, whilst the choreography of all that chaos brokered images that were reality made over.

When at last his show did end, my Loss thought to introduce herself but a few short steps had her beset by bitter disappointment. For so skilfully had he spun his tale and with such presence of mind, that no thought had my Loss given to the man behind that painted face or from whence his tales did come. But persona cast aside, his thoughts then lay bare. No longer the fearless performer that had enthralled her so but a simple man bent on his return to the silent majority. A drab tenement he called home and a life otherwise unremarkable but for the many hours he gave to an art few favoured. Hidden beneath daubed visage, the cruel and rigid lines of later years, that said much of the mournful meditation on ageing and loss.

"It is an ………illusion," he said with a doffing of his top hat and a bemused smile. But it was not to his act that he made reference and remarkable for the rarity it was my Loss simply waited for him to continue.

"You see there is nothing upon which the dealings of these times are harder than the voice that beggars moderation. Nor might anything be extoled with more rigor than the pursuit of fortune and though I have doggedly avoided both, on high days and holidays I reap riches beyond their imaginings."

My Loss saw then how that man of mimes had captured in his mind things not willingly revealed and the parodies of those voyeurs he had created as they stood idly by. But she remained somewhat befuddled by his allusions to riches and would have said so if he had not continued.

"When gain courts you, it is a fickle mistress that demands all nobler aspirations be cast aside. Promising happiness and making light of misery till in time it might be the only measure of a life spent. But if you were free today, tomorrow, to remake your world over by simply making the visible invisible, to be anything your heart desired, then that would be a life of riches beyond the measure of coin." And from his imaginings came to her that drab tenement transformed into something of much grander design.

It was only then that my little mistress of thoughts did find her voice and small was it. For she knew she had been well duped and what lay beneath that carefully crafted visage was his alone.

"Who are you ...... really?" she asked but there was more to his repertoire for without fanfare or flurry he simply reached into the very air and plucked forth a book. No rhyme or reason proffered but held out for her to take. A tale unpublished from an author that gave no name and with that he was gone.

Not a Mime Man upon his lonesome way but in the blink of an eye and inside that book two words that made more of that strange encounter.

For Loss!

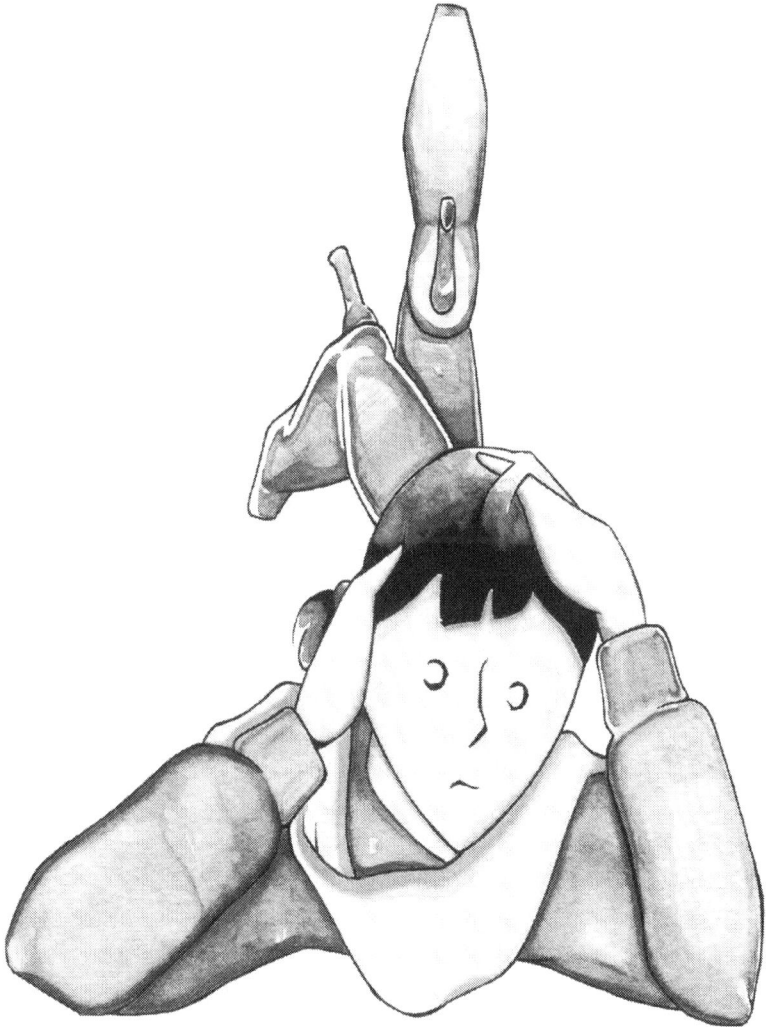

13. The Beast Within

On that mysterious book my Loss did dwell. Not reading it as one might expect, but upon its phantom origins. And though I thought it obvious that 'he' had somehow been party to its appearance, she was steadfast in decrying it so. I thought then how strange 'he' had not taken to her trail or their paths yet crossed. A thought I allowed to linger but upon which she would not be drawn and I felt the mystery that was my little Loss deepen.

In time she heard whispers of an author who had written many hundreds of books yet none had he published and so it was for that novel novelist my Loss then searched. Though not an easy man was he to find, for known not by the books he wrote yet flush with coin he had bought anonymity in an obscure district shadowed by metropolis. Where the narrow backstreets were marred by grime and secrets few cared to know were kept.

I thought it a strange setting for such prolific works to find form and wondered then if perhaps it was that same ruse woven by a certain smith of words at work. Though upon saying as much to my little sleuth she assured me there was no trickery afoot. Indeed, meeting her in that period and place with a stiffened gait and features long ravished by the relentless tramp of time, it was clear he had few vanities on which to pander, though in truth he bore this well and dapper did he present.

"Welcome, welcome," that sage of sagas proclaimed upon her arrival and with much mirth, for he knew few visitors and thought she had a bookish look about her.

A tad bedraggled from her journeys she took the chair he proffered, one of peculiar design that had it floating upon the air and warm to the touch, a yawn barely concealed as she looked to the room about her. A

full circle round with shelves from floor to ceiling with a great glass dome at its centre and as many books and more as her own beloved study had held; each perfect bound and standing as silent sentinels. But for all this, it was a mirror of monstrous proportions that held her gaze. And everything in that place so much at odds with the world beyond that there was cause to wonder if his was a charade of a different making.

"Why do you horde your words so?" my weary ranger asked.

"Why, why? So to find myself," and at this he began to trawl the books upon those shelves, his voice coming soft and low as if memories had him at a great distance. His heart and soul in a chapter not long upon the page, remembering everything yet curiously devoid of sentiment as the strangest agitation came upon him. An intrigue that had my little seer leaning towards hidden purpose in those unpublished works and much resolved to find what that might be.

"Are you lost?" she gently asked.

"No, no." He repeated for he had taken on the most infuriating habit of recapping his words. "Not now but I think we are all many things. Take myself, I am a son, a brother, but husband or father are fancies that might have been had commerce not consumed me. My lot, breathing life to the dreams of others whilst a little of myself died each day. For coin was plenty and with it I worshipped at the altar of media, reinventing myself time after time in the image of others till I no longer

recognised my own true face. Letting the words of others......define me."

"Yes, yes." My little mimic said, for she was beginning to think him a tad fey and given to rants, "but tell me of your books."

Taking a heavy tome from shelf he glanced anxiously towards that mirror and again did he drift, as though lost to a reality for his eyes only. That room seeming to become a little darker, her limbs a little heavier, as she watched him turn those pages. His fingers caressing each as though a source of manna, though in truth it was his eyes that stirred her so. Greedy and listless as though a great hunger was upon him and reaching for his thoughts she found those leaves that had him so ensnared. Not laden heavy with rich pros but images that were hers drawn forth and it was in that moment my Loss felt unseen eyes upon her. So very cold they were as to make her shudder and in the mirror a bold shadow of the beast that teller of tales had become. For his life spent on hollow pursuit it was upon the memories of others that he had come to prey.

And knowing then that chair for its wicked purpose she had presence of mind to find her feet.

Had you or I lingered it might well have been our undoing but her disc would come upon her bidding and she did want from that thief of thoughts the inspiration for such foul deeds. Seeking darkest depths that were his imaginings alone and from whence dread whispers spewed forth a name.

Slothman.

14. That Man Of Sloth

That my intrepid quester had met such dark and nefarious characters and had not baulked did truly fill me with admiration and it was with baited breath I waited upon tale of this Slothman. My thoughts inclined towards epic quest that spanned vast swathes of time but in that I was to know the bitter sting of disappointment, for his name was not unknown. More, my Loss seemed much perplexed, for the annals of that Great Hall had been much divided as to the standing his name inferred.

Decried as sinner with indifference being at the heart of the matter, proclaimed patron for a mind that had made real many fictions of science, he had foremost been a man of great reclusion. His Aerie, a tower of such phenomenal reach it might have been tethered to the stars, had his aspirations been upon so set and it was to this place then that my little seeker of truth did go. Her expectations, a mixed bag with an image of a handsome man to mind for he had been someone upon whom vanity had prevailed.

I would have had it a daunting task to gain audience with a man of such renown and that a gamut of many toadies might first be met. But sat high in his splendid isolation such fictions that he had made real had not considered the likes of Loss seeking word. Though in truth I fear she may have wished it so. For in that place she did find a pendulous and bloated thing that flew in the face of a history once written. All about him such industry as did fill his coffers filling many screens for the viewing, with him upon a throne of his own design. A crass and lurid monstrosity that barely bore his bulk, verily shouting disdain for all those below him and dangling from one outstretched hand a wooden mannequin that had him so absorbed, another rudely cast aside. Each a study in abject misery with ragged scowling face as though theirs was not a happy lot.

"How peculiar," he said to those wooden figures. "We have a visitor whose secrets dwarf my own. Shall we bid her closer?" And with that he did jiggle thumbs and fingers so as to solicit mock reply, each tiny movement a portent of gloom that did chill my Loss with a sense of the irreparable. For though she counted but one man of Sloth two minds did before her linger. One wit full of self, the other long given over to an indolence born of plenty and neither would she have treasured up.

"Tarry not," that man of sloth implored her, for he was keen to know the measure of his mysterious visitor. But there was an overwhelming malevolence in those figures that had her favouring caution and hastily did she discard such questions as she had thought to ask.

"They look very......... old." She said and seeing the object of her reticence a shadow did cross his portly chops.

"Not so," said that man of great girth with mirthless smirk, "it is a condition of their making that they do not age well. Only a few days gone that they came to me unblemished, their features smooth and alive with fresh tints. And now......?"

With question cast my Loss did closer go, seeing then a parody of age in those wizened and gnarled forms with strings so frayed it seemed to her they had been well played. Searching within for kind words, yet she would not have herself party to a lie and with but one question seeming most proper she did then enquire as to whether that puppet master had thought to name them.

"Indeed," said that merchant of sloth, looking down upon them. "Tethered to my left hand is greed, upon the floor lays witless and by their expressions they would have you think them most wronged, their twisted truths so rendered in but black or white." With these words a catalyst that transformed that aerie of sloth to but a pedestal floating above the world and below great cities reaching shore to shore. The banners of industry and technologies that made it such, numbering no more than seven. Upon each street the legacies of money changers who had brokered coin and time upon dark whispers for dreams were an easy sell. Yet more was there, for all about were people in flight. Taken to the sky en masse for that is what they craved. Not in modes of mass transportation but each in an expression of their own fancy. Seeking freedom in a world growing ever smaller, as the great wheels of commerce ever turned and of those seven banners the highest did fly upon Slothman's Aerie.

That world about then fading my Loss did stand appalled as she turned again to those mannequins. Not made from wood! But play things for a Slothman. Each bought on promises and sapped by dreams that might ever elude them and he taking much delight in the truth my Loss did see.

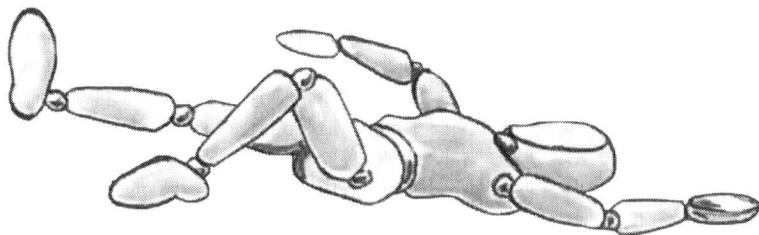

"Whilst they hanker for the more, they will peddle themselves cheap," he said without trace of malice.

"And you?" My Loss did say. "What cravings might have you selling yourself so?" But growing bored of his little visitor he had turned once more to play, leaving only darkest whispers to plague her thoughts.

15. Whisperers In The Dark

I must talk now of dark despicable creatures for it was these that had sullied my sleep and of whom my Loss then spoke. That drew about themselves the shadows of night, yet walked in sunlight with changing faces for the beguiling of those upon whom they preyed, though they would have had themselves dismissed as the fancy of fevered minds.

Dark whisperers she did call them and a shadowy society of faceless denizens were they that had ghosted in a mill of rumours spanning many centuries gone, with more beyond this now. But when I begged of her a name so that I might know these creatures of dark dealings I would have thought her about a jest had her bearing not been so solemn, for she did only know them to be once called Knowledge Ninjas. And I must

71

cry upon you to believe this disclosure did turn me disturbingly cold for you may recall I had once given thought to such as these. Skilfully weaving their way through corporate ranks, information their currency of choice and I had cause to consider then if in fact cupidity, rough trade and whinging cares had not been foremost in their thoughts. Though not my intention to demean them so, I will not deny such notion heralded a vague uncertain dread from which I could not easily turn.

"I think it a hard thing to know the true face of another." My Loss then said and though more that might have dispelled my fears she would not say, it was clear these creatures of whom she spoke were much at odds with those Knowledge Ninjas of my youth. Hers, predatory chameleons extraordinaire, mimicking that which those they sought to influence might least fear and in the telling of such I was shocked by the change that came over her. For her little face, naturally devoid the penuries of age, then seemed fraught and fallen in as though a great weariness had found her.

I thought it perhaps the memory of her encounter with those sorcerers of dark design that ailed her so or that mocking numeral now numbering two, but it was to prove my own stalwartness for which she feared. Begging of me then that second promise, my fears that such would make my first pale by comparison truly founded, my role as scribe meeting its harried end. For the course of her quest had till then been run and these trespassers of mind that might pervert knowledge and bend the strongest of wills to their bidding were such that she would not come upon them alone. My Loss seeking of me three little letters spoken freely as one and nought else could I give. For between true friends there need be no more than the word 'yes' and with that hardly passed my lips we were gone.

No sagacity of movement or temporal passage but the rapid fading of our little sanctuary and in its place that city of London finding form, encompassing us, and we at its heart in the shadow of Horatio. For of the familiar it was all that remained. No more black cabs, but automobiles without need of man that whispered on their passing and shanty all around. This city now subdued by long arm of law, so peculiar beyond my years. With I looking to the thousands about and finding a vague uncertain terror in knowing dark eyes might be upon us.

"You fear too much," my Loss said gently. "Their power lays in the cadence of words and guises; in the slight and insignificant so that it might be impossible to track their tread………don't worry so," and with that she took my hand, setting off at a lively pace. Fears for self that loitered, paling, as I wondered what I had done to be so severely tried.

Towards Old Holborn we then made our way for there abouts a whisperer of dark things lingered. Such remarks as I did hazard, to break the tedium of our trek, answered only in monosyllables as my little trekker sought that glamour wielded for common minds. Taking each

image and casting it aside till there was nowhere else for that denizen of darkness to hide. We then finding ourselves beyond the busy scenes in an obscure place where shady deals might be done and coin turned quick for those with no truck for consequence. All about us fitting prey for darker minds to be found. Not the low browed and disenfranchised but those that commerce favoured, each seeking more. Men and women, imbued with wealth and sense of self, demeanours so perfectly prescribed that we might know them well and somewhere betwixt them, a monger of mercurial design. It was aside one particularly vociferous knot of these braggers that my Loss did choose to stop. My attention drawn to a ruddy faced gentleman with monstrous chin, the meat upon him soft and sallow and me so sure we had found our mark for amiable to all did he seem. But it was for Loss to put me right. Her eyes beyond that boisterous cluster where shadows held sway over light and darkness coalesced.

"They think they know their own minds but it is an illusion they have taken to easily."

No voice giving sound to these words for they were within my head, no lips betraying their origin but with that it did come forward as a red haired rogue with cigar in hand and all the frills of calm retreat. Each step taken seeming to scatter despair and mystery in that place as tempers about us flared. Fears corralled en mass for a trend would they make and in that blinkered state such thoughts of change forever lost to thoughts of self. This Dark Whisperer now before me, its covert presence filling me with earnest dread for surely did I think our cards marked. Yet no heed to my Loss did it give. Instead, simply nodding at me as though it had been I it had been waiting for and the measure of me it would have. Not another word spoken then, but turning on heel and taking once more to the shadows as a pale light about me rose.

16. That Golden Crown

I knew then what that pale light did herald and reticent was I to acknowledge return to that solemn room. My eyes closed tight like a child intent on escaping the unwelcome. But in Kipling's shadow all men must once least follow for there comes time when childish things must be put aside and all fears embraced. All things learnt brought to fore. All ends come to pass and in the silence of my surroundings I knew this epicurean melee of a temporal odyssey that had intrigued and engaged me so would be not marked with heart felt goodbyes. No awkward place where in silence lingered, nor promises that might ease ends passing. For my little Loss was gone, only memories left to loiter and my heart a rabid creature gnawing at my breast.

All about me then a cacophony of sounds, that of industry did bellow. Of coin bartered, fortune made and the naïve assignations of youth made real. For full faculties I knew once more and so fitting a start to this tale of Loss that had found me in a bed where a broken thing might lay.

Stealing myself then for the changes about I did open my eyes, a door before me that beggared egress, a window to be flung wide and beyond that a raggedy man and I on the other side in much splendid isolation. One man, one the numeral upon that wall, and all around me another glass monolith to corporate endeavours raised by one I knew too well. But beyond these things it was to that Golden Scroll the moment went. Not ravaged by flame but before me now. Curled upon itself with ribbon cast asunder and mine for the reading. Though you may have had me fervent to read those words, I did easily stay my hand as thoughts turned once more to my little Loss and her temporal quest. Those characters of whom she had told all a nexus upon which her search had turned. Each leading to the other and I, the final link in that tortuous chain, with Dark Whisperer to me and my measure for its taking.

Knowing then this tale so near end, was but the beginning of another as yet unwritten, I took that Golden Scroll to hand. With expectations of a magic to be revealed yet finding in its stead a chase begun with words the lure, each one I came upon fading before my eyes, for so ruined no substance did they hold, until but one remained and that but for an instant as in my hands that scroll did crumble. With cruel irony of such twisted trick not upon me lost. That thought once mine to know, now again upon the wind. This then the point upon which a future I would chose and a second chance given, for it had been my first poor choice that had led Loss to me and I the better for the knowing.

"I will know it when you see it," she had said in that quirky little voice and I had been compelled to find that to which I had not been ready then to open. That same door before me now, so meagre in proportions and no hesitation in my stride for my Loss I would make proud.

Three steps did I then take, a handle did I turn and honest Ron on the other side, the tramp of time upon him. Bald palette with pigtail and teeth now capped by gold, a crass statement for new money that had risen high without care or condolences for those who had paved his way. And do not think it an easy thing to concede the failings of a parent, for in doing so it is an escapable supposition that such lacking's may find themselves passed on. For it is in the sins of a father lasting legacy may be found and in all good conscience I had sullied myself for that golden crown. Conscience caring little for dark design and in time I might have been any one of those tainted souls my Loss had come to cross. The makings of that Man of Sloth, Wordsmith and that Teller too, so easy now to see in this man who would be king and nought else could I do but collar turn to walk away. My part in this great unravelling still unknown but a new path before me as memories of lost friend lingered.

"I would ask that you write of me......... a little every day." My Loss had asked. Knowing neither pen nor keyboard came easy to a man with no time for trivial pursuits and had thought to leave a reminder. Folded neatly and placed in jacket pocket, the lingering smell of saveloy still upon it. Seven graduates, six with heads bowed down and one I could not forget. And that word lingering upon fated scroll, five simple letters spoken as one and given from the heart.

Trust.

Till next time, SJM.

ABOUT THE AUTHOR

Stephan J Myers was born in England and Loss De Plott is his debut novel.

He is currently writing the second in the series of Loss De Plott novels entitled Whisperers In The Dark, but time is a constant no one can deny and should he fail in such lofty aspirations he asks only that you never forget this tale of Loss.

In the mean time you can find out a little more about Stephan or the elusive Loss De Plott at www.StephanJMyers.com

Printed in Great Britain
by Amazon.co.uk, Ltd.,
Marston Gate.